AF407013

Kindness Has No Limit

THE MYSTERIOUS SHADOW

AUSTIN MACAULEY PUBLISHERS™
LONDON • CAMBRIDGE • NEW YORK • SHARJAH

Aamna Salem Bin Hashel

Copyright © Aamna Salem Bin Hashel (2021)

ISBN - 9789948347170 - (Paperback)
ISBN - 9789948347347 - (E-book)

Application Number: MC-10-01-3001666
Age Classification: E

First Published (2021)
AUSTIN MACAULEY PUBLISHERS FZE
Sharjah Publishing City
P.O Box [519201]
Sharjah, UAE
www.austinmacauley.ae
+971 655 95 202

إلى كل من شجعني وحثّني وساندني لإنتاج هذا الكتاب

I would like to thank my wonderful parents for encouraging me to read which then lead me to writing my own book. They'll always have a place in my heart for giving me an amazing past, present, and hopefully a bright future.

Introduction

I am Sophie Bethalion. I live with my mum, Mrs. Bethalion, my dad, Mr. Bethalion, my eight-year-old brother, James, and my five-year-old sister, Molly. My dad is a businessman; he owns a company. My mother got retired from being an engineer. We are a pretty wealthy family.

Chapter 1

The First Day of School

We just moved into town, Red Berry Hills,
because this place is closer to my dad's work,
and it's better for us to stay with him rather than
seeing him for only two days in every three months.

Today is my first day of school. I am so nervous;
there are butterflies swarming in my stomach.

I was in my room when my mum called me,
alarming me that breakfast was ready.

I walked downstairs anxiously, hoping that
school will go great for me.

I sat down on the brown, wooden, shiny chair
at the kitchen table with my mum, James, and Molly.
My dad was already at work.

SCHOOL

"Why is my sweetie not smiling today?" my mom said, concerned.
"I'm fine, Mum," I said glumly, while I was moving my spoon
in my cereal bowl without making eye contact with her.
"But you don't look fine!"

My parents didn't like us when we're feeling down, especially my mum.
"I am very nervous," I slipped these words out.
"Don't worry, sw-" my mum replied to me,
but I interrupted, "What if my teachers are strict?
What if people bully me? What if I have no friends?"
It was like I could tell some of my future.

"As I told you yesterday, answering the same questions,"
my mum spoke, "teachers can be strict,
but if you behave well, then you'll be fine.
And don't worry, you will have friends,
this is the third time I'm telling you this!"
And about the bullies," my mum continued,
"why don't you teach them to be as sweet as honey, like you?"

She shot out these words confidently with a smile.
She stood up, came over to me, and bent down to kiss me
on the cheek. She waved me a goodbye. "Your bus is here, sweetie."

She heard my school bus honking outside;
I didn't hear the bus because of the short conversation
we were having. I was buried deep into it.
"Love you, Mum, James, and Molly!"
I said, shutting the door behind me.

When I entered the bus, it wasn't silent at all.
Instead, I was in a wild forest. When I got to sit on my seat,
I stared outside, looking through the window.

"Brooklyn, your pink hair is amazing!" one exulted.
"Yeah, Brooklyn, your hair is stunning!"
another one spoke.
"I surely do know!" showed off Brooklyn,
sounding like an evil drama queen.

Chapter 2

What's That Shadow?

We only past a few blocks and then I suddenly saw a shadow
of someone in a narrow path between two brick buildings,
but it suddenly faded in a blink of an eye.
I thought I was imagining things,
so I shrugged and continued admiring the nature outside.

The bus picked up a few more people but
none of them were interested in sitting beside me,
they definitely knew each other from the past year
or so. I sat down alone for the whole journey quietly,
realizing I have never been this quiet for that
amount of time before. When we reached school,
I was able to reach my classroom and meet my
teacher with the help of an assistant,
but I didn't get to know anyone yet.

It was awkward sitting alone for the whole school day.
Even at break times, I would sit abandoned,
eating my snack or lunch with my back to a tree trunk.
When the bell rang for the sake of it being the end of the
school day, the school doors were bashed open with all the
students looking like an untidy army ready to battle.
When I hopped on the bus,
I sat on the same seat as I did in the morning,
still without a figure beside me.

Finally, the bus dropped me home. Sighing a sigh of relief,
I entered the house. My dad was still at work,
but my mum and siblings were home.
My mum obviously asked me how my day was with
a smile on her face.
I smiled back, put my head down and murmured,
"It wasn't that good."

I had to tell her the truth, but I felt and knew that she wasn't
expecting that answer, to the point that her gorgeous smile turned
invisible."But why, Hun?"
she asked worryingly. My mum hated the sight of sadness;
she is a positive young lady, and I am wanting and trying to be like her.

I told her that I was alone the whole day and nobody even came
towards me to shoot out a two-letter word which is 'Hi!'
My mom listened to me respectfully without interrupting.
Her response was a pleasing smile. She kneeled down and held my hands,
coming closer to my ear. She began whispering,
"Everything will change, trust me."
I looked at her, with her doing the same thing.

Later that day, my dad entered with a joyful,"Good evening!"
I, my mother, and two of my siblings greeted him happily which
made my dad look even more delighted.
We had pasta for dinner and I loved that.
It was so mouth-watering seeing that red bloody sauce
sliding down and dressing those long strings!

We started eating and Dad asked the same question
Mum asked me when I came from school. My answer was the same and
my dad was disappointed because I wasn't that happy.

He then said positively, "Everything will change."
Noticing that he said the same thing as my mum,
I stayed sitting there without a word, not
opening the doors of my mouth. I then nodded.
When my stomach got blocked because of me being full,
I wiped my mouth with a napkin and stood up,
putting my empty plate in the dishwasher.

"Do you want anything else, Soph?" my mum asked.
"No. Thanks Mum," I replied.
I then went upstairs to my bedroom to take a warm shower,
since I was quite exhausted from a long day.
It was relieving and relaxing.
When I got out of the shower,
I felt amazingly radiant. I felt tired,
so I went to kiss my parents on the cheek with
a goodnight, hid myself under the covers, and slept.

Chapter 3

Seeing the Shadow Again

The next day, I woke up as usual. I forced myself to get out of bed, all
grumpy and grouchy, and went ahead to the bathroom.
After that, I went downstairs with a slight smile on my face.
I felt sleepy. My mother hurried me up to eat breakfast so
that I won't be late to school and have to go with an empty stomach.

My two siblings were looking happy. They were eating their pancakes
that had shiny maple syrup drizzled on them.
I always wonder how they look excited in the morning.
After I was done with breakfast,
I still had time until the bus would arrive,
so I sat down and read the book that I was reading.
The bus then suddenly honked outside,
and I put the book that I was reading in my bag because
since I knew I'll be alone for the whole day in school,
I could read, instead of me doing just completely
nothing but staring at people. They might think I had gone nuts!

I went over to the bus and sat at the same place as
yesterday. I hated sitting isolated! All of a sudden,
about a few blocks away,
I noticed that shadow again, but this time,
I was able to see who it was.

Chapter 4

What's That Shadow?

I saw a girl standing beside the gigantic garbage can...
"Who is she?" I began to mutter to myself,
tilting my head with confusion.
Later that day, at break-time,
I sat down with the tree trunk behind my back again.

I was thinking about that girl for the entire time,
just asking myself questions.
What was she doing there?
For how long has she been there?
But most importantly, *Why was she there?*
This question sent chills down my spine;
it made my brain cells twist and my mind generators turn.

My unstoppable questions that had a mysterious and
unknown answer were interrupted by the noisy bell ringing.
I picked up my bag which was surprisingly open.
All of my belongings in my school bag shot down towards
the green and fresh-looking grass. I gathered all of my things,
concerned about how my backpack's zipper was wide open,
only when I heard giggles coming from
the other side of the tree trunk.

When I looked behind the tree trunk to see who this person was,
I saw Brooklyn, the popular but mean girl in school.

I knew that it was her straightaway because
I heard about her when I was in the school bus,
as they described her dying her hair pink.
She pointed at me and shouted, "LOSER!"

I looked at her, giving her an annoyed look.
I was so mad, but didn't say anything.
I was way too nervous to speak.

Chapter 5

Meeting the Source of the Shadow

A few days later, I woke up with it snowing so badly.
I checked my alarm clock and it was 7:30 a.m. I panicked,
moving nonstop like a monkey, not being able to sit still.

I was so frustrated because my mum didn't wake me up
for school, telling me that I was running late.
I hurried to the bathroom, wore my school uniform and
went to check on my siblings, but they
were still sleeping.
When I went downstairs, I didn't see my mum.
It was ordinary that my dad wasn't home, he was at work.
But not seeing my mum was strange.

I started calling out for her only when all of a sudden,
my eyes caught sight of a remarkable folded note
on the living-room table.
I picked it up and it said:

*Your school has sent us an email, saying that you have the day off
because of the bad weather. Take care of your younger siblings! I'm
currently at a friend's house due to her illness.
Love, your mum. x*

I sighed a sigh of relief and planted a smile on my face.
I hated the fact that I had nobody to hang out with at school anyway,
so that was a bonus point! In addition to that,
the weekend's approaching, and knowing that it's on its way
was a heads up too! I wanted to go outside because I remembered
that shadow. I wanted to go out to see if the shadow was still there,
and I wanted to know who the source of the shadow was.

I knew the shadow was there because it was approximately
the same time the school bus comes to pick me up,
except it's just 15 minutes later.
I then thought about James and Molly,
but I was 100% sure that they weren't going to wake up.
I changed to a cozy winter outfit and stepped outside.

Going out there, I felt like I turned into an ice cube.
It was still snowing, but I would never refuse an interesting adventure.
I started walking whilst I was cuddled in my coat,
with the whistling of the cold wind dancing around me.
I then suddenly coughed with the ability
to see my breath escaping my mouth.

Throughout my walking journey, I saw nobody around me.
It felt like I was walking in a haunted mansion's corridor,
but outdoors. Leaving deep footprints behind me
made me realize how much it had snowed.
I mustn't have left the house, but I really wanted some answers
to my questions instead of leaving myself hanging.
When I reached the position where the shadow always was,
I didn't see anyone. Not even the shadow. I began to shake,
not because of the cold, but because of the fact that
I might be imagining which made me petrified, but it wasn't possible.

I walked for a few steps only, on my way back home,
with my head down without looking back. Abruptly,
I heard a voice speak out. A soft and pure voice.
I stood still like a mannequin, and lifted my head, confused.
I then turned my head and found myself with my eyes wide open;
they were the size of a tennis ball.
"Hi," she began to say, waving at me. I was quiet.

Chapter 6

Who is this Girl?

I saw a girl with dirt on her face;
she was wearing dusty, torn clothes in this cold weather.
I saw her eyeballs point downwards.

I was speechless, but then somehow managed
to spill some words out of my mouth.
"Um. Hey," I waved back too, also looking down.
"My name is Carla."
"Nice to meet you, Carla. I am Sophie."
"Nice to meet you too, Sophie."

There was an awkward silence right after this
short conversation for a few seconds.

I and Carla were staring at each other,
with a couple of blinks here and there.
I wanted to break the silence,
so I asked her one of the questions that
I wanted an answer to, but with regret…

"Um, Carla?" I started. She had a tiny smile on her face.
And I just realized that her eyes were gorgeous.

"Yes?" she said softly.
"Why are you here every day?"
Her smile was lost. I began to gulp.
"I'm sorry! It's just–"
"It's okay. I understand," she spoke.
I stayed still.

Supermarket

She sighed sadly and started to let out some words.
"We are a poor family, and I come here to get leftover
food that I find by the garbage can to take to
my mum and brother."
"The food shouldn't even be thrown,
it's such a waste and risky to be eaten,"
I muttered to myself.
There was a moment of silence,
but then she continued, "My father…"

She stayed quiet. I saw a tear roll down her cheek.
"He passed away three months ago."
I felt so sad that I started to tear up too.
"I'm so sorry."
"It's okay, don't be sorry, but I have to go. I'm ravenous,
and I bet my mum and brother are too."
"No, don't eat that. Here, have this."

I took out some coins out of my pocket and lent them to her.
"Go buy something, and I'll come with you."
"No, I can't take that," she replied.

"Come on. Take it, for me." I started to smile.
She blushed. Her cheeks turned as red as an elegant rose.
"Thank you," she said quietly.

Carla and I went to the only known '24-hours open'
supermarket in Red Berry Hills.
It was only a five-minute walk, but it was harder because
of the snow that was still pouring from the sky.

We went to the cashier and there was change left.
Carla wanted to give it back to me, but I refused.
"Keep it."
She nodded.

I offered some help by carrying the bag,
but she didn't let me because I have already done
so many nice things to her."Kindness has no limit, Carla."

She looked at me, but still didn't let me carry the bag. I giggled.
On the way back, we started talking until we reached
the narrow path where the garbage can was.

"I'll come to you at 8:00 a.m. tomorrow. Will you be awake?"
"Of course I'll be awake! I hate waking up late!"
"Really? Me too!"

We high-fived each other with a chuckle.
"Have a nice day!" I said happily, waving to her.
"Same to you!" she replied.
Walking back home, I was still freezing,
but I was glad I had a friend now.

When I arrived, it was 9:30 a.m. My siblings were awake,
watching T.V. in the living room.

"Where were you?" James asked.
"Did you eat breakfast?" I didn't want to answer his question,
so I changed the subject.
"No," he said, shaking his head.

"Well, I guess you and Molly would like some cereal?"
"Yes, please!" they both shouted at the same time.
I went to the kitchen and made their breakfast ready.
"James, Molly, breakfast is ready!"
"We are coming!" they shouted excitedly.

I was able to tell that they were starving,
so I decided to apologize.
"I'm sorry for not making breakfast ready for you
as soon as you woke up."
"Oh yeah, about that, where did you say you were?"

"Umm. I...I was in...sorry, I need to use the toilet!"
I rushed upstairs to my bedroom and read a book to pass time.
My siblings already know where to put their dishes after
every meal, so I wasn't worried.

Later that evening, my parents were already home.
We were having vegetable soup with a salad plate for dinner.
I was so happy that I now have a friend, so I wanted to tell
my parents about it. "Mum, Dad,
I have good news for you!"

"Yes, honey?" my mum said cheerfully.
"We would love to hear some good news, sweetie!"
my dad added with a smile.

"Well, I have a new friend!"
"That sounds great! Patience is the key!"

I nodded with a smile and continued eating.
After three seconds exactly, my mum started speaking,
"Wait a minute, how can you have a friend when
you had the day off today? I bet it's not the neighbors
because it was snowing."

My mum was confused, and so was my dad,
as I can read his face.
Both of my siblings were drinking their soup and
eating their salad without paying attention to our conversation.
I felt guilty. I didn't expect the conversation to
lead to this path. I had no choice but to tell them.
I told them the whole story from beginning to end.
They were listening.

"I don't blame you for being adventurous.
I used to be like you when I was younger,
but I have never left the house without permission, and
you better have not done that. Don't do that again, sweetie,
it's dangerous!"

"Yes, Mum. I'm sorry."
"Take me to that girl tomorrow," my dad bellowed.
I wrinkled my eyebrows in confusion.
My mom was confused too, I was able to tell.
"You heard me."
"What are you talking about?"
"Just wait until tomorrow."
It was a few minutes past my bedtime anyways,
because I was chatting with my parents about Carla.
But I kissed my parents on their cheeks,
went to take a shower, and flew straight onto my bed.

Chapter 7

My Dad Meets Carla's Family

The next day, I went downstairs, and my parents were already
awake. It was 8:30 a.m., and my breakfast
was a peanut-butter-and-jelly sandwich which I adored!

Right after I put in the last mouthful of my sandwich,
my dad demanded that I hop in his car. I did.

When I got in the car, he asked me where
I saw Carla every day. I told him that it only took
five minutes to reach there when I walked, unlike driving.

I lead him on the way required. We got out of the car and
she was there sitting on a large brick.

"Hello, Carla!" my dad said cheerfully to her.
I waved whilst she smiled to both of us, waving back.
"How are you doing?" he asked her.
"Pretty good," she replied.

"Sophie, I was waiting for you since 8:00 a.m.
Why didn't you show up?"
"Oops! Sorry! I forgot!" I uttered. My dad chuckled.

"My daughter, Sophie, told us about you, and I thought
I'd come to meet you and your mother.
Can we see her?"
Carla said that she'll check and come back.
She came back and nodded, sticking her thumb up.
We followed her to her house. There was no house.

Her mother was sitting on an old medium-sized
beige piece of cloth with stains.
Her younger brother was sleeping with
his head on her lap.

Carla went to stand beside her mother
with her hands behind her back.
"Hello, madam," my dad beamed.
"Hello," her mother smiled.
I stayed quiet.

My dad and Carla's mum had a nice chat for a while.
I didn't really know what they were talking about since
I went to play with Carla.
20 minutes later, my dad called me,
telling me that we'll have to go.

I wanted to stay and play with Carla because
we were having tons of fun."Can I stay, please?"

"Sorry honey, but we have to go."
I nodded.
My dad went to start the car engine.
"Goodbye, Carla."
"Goodbye, Sophie."

I walked towards the car, hopped in, and
pulled the window down.
"Bye, Carla!" I yelled whilst my dad was
already moving the car.
"Bye, Sophie!" she yelled back.
My dad honked as he left.

When we arrived home, my dad had a severe
talk with my mum, but I knew nothing.

Chapter 8

Surprising Carla's Family

About two months later which passed
by as fast as lighting, Carla and I were still friends,
and I knew a couple of kids at school. But when
I came home from school one day,
I saw my dad summoning me towards his car.

"What's going on?" I asked.
He had a grin on his face. I was puzzled.
"Where's Mum and my siblings?"

His grin was still in sight, but he was still muted. I got into the
car and sighed looking outside the window. After driving for ten
minutes, my dad stopped by a single-story villa; it looked
beautiful.

My mum and siblings were there, standing in the yard.
I got out of the car and hugged my mum,
squeezing her tightly. But when I looked back,
my dad's car had vanished already.

"Mum, why are we here? And where is Dad going?"
"Dear, this is a surprise for Carla, her mother,
and her little brother. Your dad is going to pick
them up and surprise them."

My mouth opened in shock, and all of a sudden,
it turned into a ginormous smile.
My dad arrived, and looking through the car window,
I could already tell from Clara's face that she was surprised.

I ran to hug her and then my dad finally spoke,
"Madam, this is now yours."
She began to mutter words, "Wha...hang on...wait."
My dad chortled and she stood for a second,
"Am I dreaming?"

"I am determined that you're not!"
my dad approved with a titter.
Then, Carla's mum went to hug my mother, with tears
of happiness rolling down her cheeks
with tears of happiness rolling down her cheeks.

Carla sprinted and hugged my dad as he picked her up
and then she came to hug me.
My mum began to give them a tour of the whole
house since it was already furnished by my parents.

After the tour, my dad announced
something that made Carla's mum rejoice.

"I have a list of jobs for you to sign up for, but no matter
what, I'm going to pay the electricity and water bills, and
put your children in school."

That was the best day of my life, and now,
Carla and I are best friends, in the same class,
and we both have lots of friends in school and out
because of how nice we've been.

Brooklyn even lost some of her friends for being mean,
but now I'm friends with Brooklyn because
she now teleported to being nicer.

I then reflected on what my mum told me
on the first day of school, "And about the bullies,
why don't you teach them to be
as sweet as honey, like you?"

"Kindness Has No Limit."

—Aamna Salem Bin Hashel·